Savannah's Savings Jar

Chelsea Addison

Illustrated by Laura Daogaru

I'll never forget the first time I met Chelsea Addison. We were at church and US Senator Cory Booker was visiting to encourage people to vote in an upcoming election. After his speech, a few of us went to an adjacent hallway to greet Sen. Booker and take photos. Then, seemingly out of nowhere, Chelsea approached me and introduced herself. She explained how she was a recent transplant to St. Louis via the Teach for America program. More importantly, she was looking for a mentor and asked me if I would consider obliging.

How could I refuse? I could tell immediately that once she identified a goal, she pursued it relentlessly. As I got to know her over the next several years, I discovered that she applied that same vigor to everything. She finished graduate school, ran for school board and won, started a successful art business, and now this series of books.

If children learn nothing else from Savannah, it should be how she saves her money and changes her habits to become financially responsible. Savannah diligently pursues her dreams with reckless abandon, asks for support when in need, and makes the necessary changes to still reach her goals. Just like Chelsea.

Savannah's Savings Jar *teaches children the valuable lessons of hard work, delayed gratification, making wise choices, and to learn from your mistakes. As the Treasurer, I started programs to teach children these very same lessons about money. I hope this book is able to convey these important values for many years to come.*

Tishaura O. Jones
Treasurer, City of St. Louis, Missouri

WHAT DO YOU KNOW ABOUT SAVING MONEY?

WHAT DO YOU KNOW ABOUT STARTING YOUR OWN BUSINESS?

WHAT ARE EXPENSES?

DO YOU SAVE YOUR MONEY?

WHAT IS A BUDGET?

WHAT IS A FINANCIAL GOAL?

Hi friends!

I'm Savannah, and this is my **savings jar**.
Recently, my friends started calling me
Saving Savannah, but it wasn't always this way.

Want to find out why?

"*Clase*, we were awarded a grant from Financial Friends! Each of you will be given start-up money for your business project."

We reviewed our lesson on being an entrepreneur before getting started!

"Remember *clase*, all of you can become entrepreneurs. You can start your own

business, or you can collaborate and start a joint venture with someone else. It's all up to you!"

Our first assignment was to create a business plan and decide on a financial goal. My financial goal was to make a $300 profit. Most of my classmates wanted to start a joint venture, but I wanted to work alone.

Do you like to work alone like Savannah, or do you prefer to work in groups? Why or why not?

I THOUGHT ABOUT WHAT KIND OF BUSINESS I WANTED TO START.

Señora Romero told me I could make money with the skills I already had, but I still had a difficult time deciding.

I wanted to start a personalized pillow company, but I didn't know how to sew.

I thought about starting a lemonade stand, but I am allergic to lemons.

I love stuffed animals, but I didn't know the first thing about making a lion from scratch!

Then, I thought about what my friends like and what they would want to buy.

Hmmmm . . .

Do you have any skills to start a business? What are they?

ALL OF A SUDDEN, I HAD AN AHA MOMENT!

I was going to create SLIME! It's fun, easy, simple, and it is popular.
I named the business Terrific Slimerrific! *Pretty cool, right?*

I had an AWESOME time starting my slime business and being the boss.

I created a budget based on my expenses. I bought very simple materials that did not cost a lot. I began to make the slime and package it in containers for my customers.

I made all sorts of slime: slime with a scent, slime in different colors; I even made glitter slime.

Terrific Slimerrific Budget and Expenses

Money I need / Startup costs
Ingredients = $133.00
Terrific Slimerrific Booth = $50.00
Total = $183.00

Recurring Costs
Ingredients = $133.00

Money I spent
$183.00 − $183.00 = $0

Imagine that you had the opportunity to start any business. What would it be?

Before I knew it, three days went by and I sold 27 jars of slime for $5.00 each! I made so much money. It was exciting to have earned my own money by making something fun and simple. Now, all I could think about was shopping!

*How much money
did Savannah make
in three days?*

*What do you like
to purchase with
your money?*

That weekend, my best friend Spencer and I went to the mall.

"Hey Spencer, look at these shoes and this hat. They would be so cute with my outfit!"

Spencer agreed, "Those are cool. You know what? My shoes are old and I could use some new ones. Why don't you buy the hat, and get both of us a pair of shoes?"

"I don't know Spencer. The hat is $30 and the shoes are $40 EACH! I really want to save my money."

Spencer rolled his eyes, "Oh Savannah, your business is doing well! Plus, with all of the money you made with Terrific Slimerrific, you have enough money to buy everything. Just save the money you don't spend."

I thought about his words, "I guess you're right. Okay, I'll get them. Hurry, quick before I change my mind!"

By the time we left the mall, I spent $110, but I still had money to put in my savings jar!

Do the math.

How much money does Savannah have left to put in her savings jar after leaving the mall?

What do you think will happen next?

I could hear Spencer bragging, "Yep, that's right. My very best friend in the whole wide world bought me these at the mall yesterday."

Everybody loved our shoes. Keisha came over to me and said, "Savannah, your shoes are so cool, I wish I had enough money to buy those."

I was basking in the moment, until Liam sneeringly stated, "How DID you have enough money to buy those shoes anyway Savannah? I hope you didn't use the money for your business! It's better to spend your money wisely when saving for a financial goal!"

"Well," I said, "If you must know. I had enough money to buy them because I made $135 selling slime!"

My friend Rachel seemed concerned, "Liam is right Savannah. You might want to check your budget to make sure you have enough money to continue your business. Maybe you should talk to Señora Romero."

What is the problem in this part of the story?

I nervously walked over to Señora Romero's desk because I didn't know what to expect.

Savannah: "Señora Romero, do you think I spent too much at the mall?"

Señora Romero: "It depends, how much money did you spend at the mall?"

Savannah: "I spent $110.00, but I was able to put $25.00 in my savings jar! I completely forgot about my budget and the list of expenses I made when I started the business!"

Señora Romero: "Well Savannah, according to your expense list, it will cost $133 to keep selling slime to your customers for Terrific Slimerrific."

Savannah: "Are you saying I don't have enough money for supplies, even with the money I saved?"

Señora Romero: "Yes. Unfortunately, you will not be able to continue with your business unless you have $133, Savannah. Remember, your budget and expenses include the cost it takes to continue selling slime to your customers. While I am happy you were thinking about saving your money, you didn't save enough to cover your expenses and continue making slime."

I WENT BACK TO MY SEAT AND WAS DEVASTATED.

How can Savannah reach her financial goal if she didn't have enough money to cover her expenses?

How do you think Savannah felt when she found out she hadn't saved enough money? How do you know?

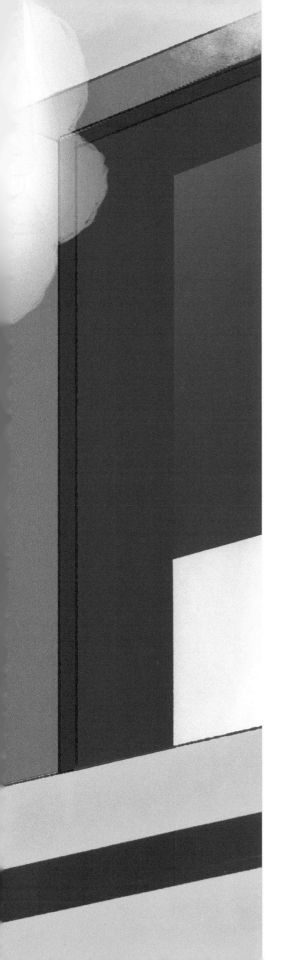

All I could think about on the bus ride home was Señora Romero's question, and how I carelessly spent my earnings instead of saving.

My parents taught me to always save at least 25% of my earnings before spending, but I didn't listen.

I was still **distraught** when I arrived home, but the smell of my mom's special lasagna made me feel better.

Mom: "Hi beautiful. Dinner is ready. I made your favorite!"

Savannah: "Daddy, I'm disappointed in myself."

Dad: "What happened, sweetheart?"

Savannah: "I don't have enough money to cover my business expenses, nor did I take your advice and save 25% of what I earned. Instead, Spencer and I went to the mall. I bought both of us new shoes and a hat for myself."

Mom: "Savannah, what did I tell you about hanging out with Spencer? We don't call him 'Spending Spencer' for nothin'! What did your teacher say?"

Savannah: "Señora Romero told me I didn't save enough money to continue Terrific Slimerrific! I wish I would have checked my budget and expenses before I spent the money. I decided not to do a joint venture because I wanted to work alone. Now, I have to figure out how to save the business all by myself. It's over!"

Dad: "No it isn't, sweetheart. I will take you to the mall after dinner. We can start to solve this problem by trying to return your hat and new shoes to get a refund."

Why do you think Mom doesn't want Savannah to hang out with Spencer?

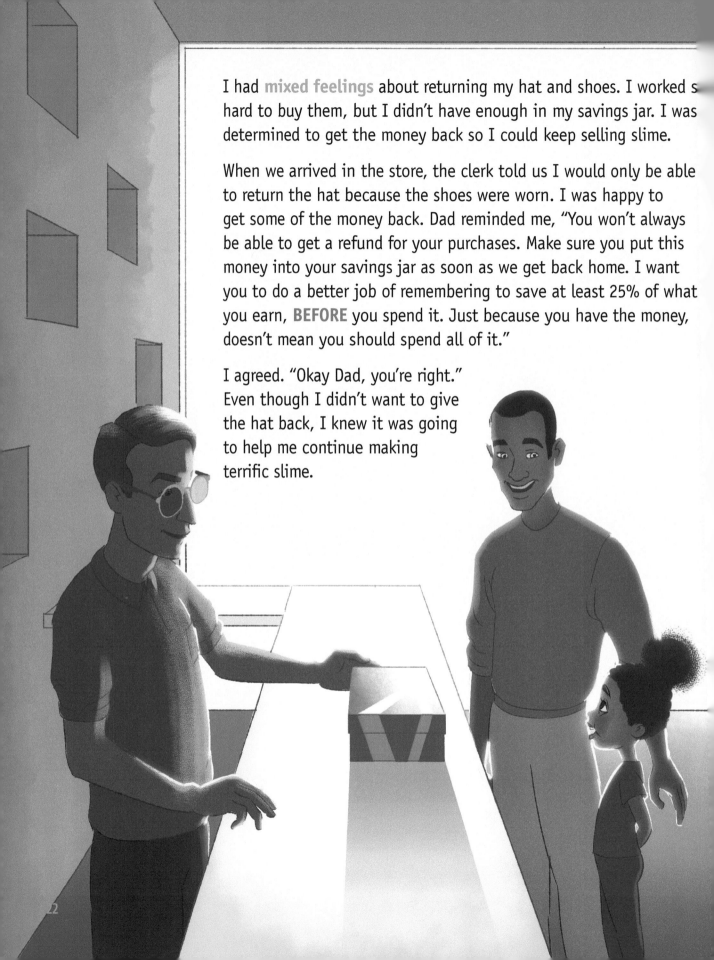

I had mixed feelings about returning my hat and shoes. I worked s hard to buy them, but I didn't have enough in my savings jar. I was determined to get the money back so I could keep selling slime.

When we arrived in the store, the clerk told us I would only be able to return the hat because the shoes were worn. I was happy to get some of the money back. Dad reminded me, "You won't always be able to get a refund for your purchases. Make sure you put this money into your savings jar as soon as we get back home. I want you to do a better job of remembering to save at least 25% of what you earn, BEFORE you spend it. Just because you have the money, doesn't mean you should spend all of it."

I agreed. "Okay Dad, you're right." Even though I didn't want to give the hat back, I knew it was going to help me continue making terrific slime.

*What did you
learn from this part
of the story?*

*What do you think will
happen next?*

23

57% 🔋

•••••📶

Savannah: Hey Spencer... I tried to return my shoes, but I could only get a refund for the hat.

Spencer:
... You did what? WHY?

I wasn't going to have enough money to continue the business. Luckily, I have $54 because I saved 25% of my birthday money.

Spencer: So what are you going to do with the money?

Savannah: Well, I am going to save 25% of the $84* and put it in my savings jar. Then, I am going to use the rest to buy more materials.

*$54 + $30 refund = $84. 25% of $84 = $21 to put
in her savings jar. Savannah has $63 for materials.

Spencer: Well, sounds like a good idea, but that's still a long way off. Don't you need $133?

Savannah: Yes I do, but it is a start.

Spencer: I am going to call you Saving Savannah! It's cool how you never give up, you'll figure it out.

Savannah: Thanks. See you at school.

Spencer: Okay see you!

Savannah: Good night.

I went to sleep proud of myself for returning the hat. I had a new plan. I was going to rebuild Terrific Slimerrific by spending my money wisely and saving as much as I could.

Why do you think Savannah saved 25% of her money instead of using all of it to purchase supplies? What happened in this part of the story?

The next day, Señora Romero introduced a new student to the class.

"*Clase*, this is Marvin. He is from Tulsa, Oklahoma, and the newest addition to our class."

I asked Señora Romero, "Can Marvin be my partner? I want to stick to my plan of rebuilding Terrific Slimerrific, and last night I realized that successful businesses take a team."

"Of course, Savannah. *Excelente* idea. Marvin, please take a seat next to Savannah. *Clase*, you have the rest of the period to continue working on your businesses."

Marvin knew a lot about money. He told me it was a habit to keep his money in jars at home. He had spending, savings, sharing, and investing jars at home! Marvin knew a lot more about money than I did! I was grateful Marvin made an investment in the business. With his investment, we had the $133 needed to cover the expenses for Terrific Slimeriffic.

Why do you think successful businesses take a team?

After a few weeks of selling slime, I renamed Marvin 'MONEY MARVIN' because with his help, Terrific Slimerrific earned $805 dollars! Our income was more than enough money to cover future expenses. There was a profit* of $622. Even after Marvin received his return on investment, I still made more than my financial goal!

We were able to grow the business by adding equipment and hiring staff to help sell even more slime.

The best part was being able to save more than 25% of my earnings and put it in my savings jar.

*Profit formula: Money earned minus the start-up cost.
$805 ($5 x 161 jars of slime) minus $183 (start-up cost) = $622 profit.

How has Savannah changed from the beginning of the story?

What valuable lesson did she learn?

A NOTE FROM SAVANNAH

When I first started saving, I didn't have a lot of money to put in my savings jar. I began a business and learned how to use my money wisely by saving at least 25% of my earnings **BEFORE** I spent it. Every time I added money to my savings jar the money increased, and I was closer to reaching my financial goal!

Do you have a savings jar? If not, create one today!

Consider saving money you receive as a gift or your allowance to reach a financial goal. Remember to save at least 25% of your money in order to have enough money to reach your financial goal.

Good luck and have fun saving!

Will you start saving your money? If so, how much?

HOW TO MAKE

WHAT YOU NEED:

- School glue
- Borax (sodium tetraborate)
- Food coloring (optional)
- Water
- Two bowls
- Stir stick

WHAT YOU DO:

1. In one bowl mix 1 oz. glue (about ¼ of the glue bottle) and ¼ cup water. If you want colored slime, add food coloring to the glue and water mixture. Lift some of the solution out of the container with the stir stick and note what happens.

2. Add ¼ cup of sodium tetraborate (Borax) solution to the glue and water mixture and stir slowly.

3. The slime will begin to form immediately. Lift some of the solution with the stir stick and observe how the consistency has changed from Step 1.

4. Stir as much as you can, then dig in and knead it with your hands until it gets less sticky. This is a messy experience but is necessary because it allows the two compounds to bond completely. Don't worry about any leftover water in the bowl; just pour it out.

5. When not in use, store the slime in a plastic bag in the fridge to keep it from growing mold.

WHY DOES THIS HAPPEN?

The glue has an ingredient called polyvinyl acetate, which is a liquid polymer. The borax links the polyvinyl acetate molecules to each other, creating one large, flexible polymer. This kind of slime will get stiffer and more like putty the more you play with it. Experiment with different glues to see if they create slime (e.g., carpenter glue, tacky glue, etc.).

Source: Familyeducation.com

Glossary

Basking - to enjoy what is going on in a situation

Budget - a plan for the amount of money available, income, and expenses

Business Plan - a detailed written plan that describes how to achieve a business idea (product or service) and the estimated expenses, revenue, and profits

Collaborate - to work with other people

Customers - people who purchase goods or services

Devastated - to feel overwhelmed, to be very sad

Distraught - very nervous and worried; having doubt or painful feelings

Earn - to gain or receive money as a result of doing a service or selling a good

Earnings - the amount of profit that a business or individual makes

Entrepreneur - someone who organizes to start, manage, and take the financial risks of a business

Equipment - a tool or machine needed to perform a task

Expenses - the cost or amount of something spent on goods or services

Financial goal - a target set to achieve for future monetary needs

Grant - a sum of money given by an organization or government for a particular pupose.

Hiring - to employ someone to do a particular job for money or other reward

Income - money received from working

Increased - to make something grow, to become more, or make greater

Investment - the act or process of putting money to work with the expectation of receiving a profit

Joint venture - a business with two or more people, companies or organizations

Personalized - to create or make something specific to someone personal likeness

Profit - earnings gained after expenses

Recurring Costs - repeated costs for each item produced or each service performed.

Refund - money paid back to a customer when a good is returned; a customer may receive a refund if he/she is not satisfied

Return on Investment (ROI) - the amount of profit an investment generate relative to its cost.

Saving - money not spent and set aside or invested for later

Skill - perform a task well because of practice or training

Sneeringly - to talk about or look at someone in a disapproving or disrespectful and unkind way

Staff - people who work on a project or job

Start-up money - the amount of money required to spend in order to start a new business or project (also referred to as seed money or start-up capital)

Phrases

From scratch - something created from the beginning without having any prior work done using anything that already exists

Mixed feelings - Emotionally confused; feeling partly positive and partly negative at the same time, in reaction to something

Spanish Terms

Clase - Class

Excelente - Excellent

Señora - Mrs.

HELLO,

While teaching second grade, I asked my students what they wanted to learn about. A lot of suggestions were lobbed around until one of my students suggested we learn about money. The class went nuts. Turns out they were all interested in learning about money. Especially this little girl, whose family bread winner had just lost her job. The kids went to recess and I started to Google financial education. There was very little for elementary school students. A lightning bolt came out of the blue and I decided to write this book. This has been a labor of love for all the children who want a hand up in understanding how to get money, how to use it and how to keep it. This is for you.

Thank you for reading *Savannah's Savings Jar*. I hope you found it helpful. Your feedback is important to me, so I hope you will please take a few minutes to write a brief review on Amazon.

I'd love to hear from you. Contact me at chelsea@financialfriendsbooks.com.

— Chelsea —

ISBN: 978-0-578-21220-3

Illustrations by Laura Daogaru
Book design: Peggy Nehmen, n-kcreative.com

For information about special sales, please contact the author:
Chelsea Addison, chelsea@financialfriendsbooks.com financialfriendsbooks.com

Published by Addwin Publishing & Media, LLC. Printed in the United States of America.

THANKS TO MY FIRST AND SECOND GRADERS
WHO INSPIRED ME TO WRITE THIS STORY!

CPSIA information can be obtained
at www.ICGtesting.com
Printed in the USA
LVHW072247260722
724506LV00007B/14